Slam Dunk Series

MUGGSY
Makes an Assist

Tess Eileen Kindig
Illustrated by Joe VanSeveren

SAINT LOUIS

For my husband, Eric,
who knew I would write for kids when I didn't know it
myself. Thanks for believing in me

Slam Dunk Series
Sixth Man Switch
Spider McGhee and the Hoopla
Zip, Zero, Zilch
Muggsy Makes an Assist

All Scripture quotations, unless otherwise indicated, are taken from the HOLY BIBLE, NEW INTERNATIONAL VERSION®. NIV®. Copyright © 1973, 1978, 1984 by International Bible Society. Used by permission of Zondervan Publishing House. All rights reserved.

Copyright © 1999 Tess Eileen Kindig
Published by Concordia Publishing House
3558 S. Jefferson Avenue, St. Louis, MO 63118-3968
Manufactured in the United States of America

Library of Congress Cataloging-in-Publication Data
Kindig, Tess Eileen.
    Muggsy Makes an Assist/ Tess Eileen Kindig.
    p. cm. -- (Slam dunk series)
    Summary: Mickey gets a chance to replace an injured teammate as a starter for the Pinecrest Flying Eagles basketball team, but trouble with the coach means that he may not continue to play.
ISBN 0-570-07018-X
    [1.Basketball--Fiction. 2.Christian life--Fiction.] I.Title.

PZ7.K5663 Mu 2000
[Fic]--dc21

99-046932

1 2 3 4 5 6 7 8 9 10   08 07 06 05 04 03 02 01 00 99

4.99

Contents

1

A Fall Is All

"Ouch!" Trish Riley cried from the far corner of the supermarket parking lot. "That hurt!"

I sighed and went over to see what was the matter *this time*. The Pinecrest Flying Eagles basketball players and cheerleaders were selling Christmas trees to raise money for new uniforms. Everyone agreed it would be lots more fun than peddling candy bars. Everyone except Trish Riley, that is. She'd been whining like a gnat ever since the truck from the tree farm pulled into the lot.

"What's wrong *now*?" I snapped. All she had to do was put price tags on a pile of trees. It wasn't rocket science.

"These needles are like daggers," she complained. "They're worse than getting shots." She sucked on her sore finger and glared at me.

"That's a Colorado blue spruce. Of course it's going to hurt. Maybe that's why gloves were invented," I told her. I'd really listened when the tree guy showed us all the different kinds of trees and told us how to take care of them. Coach

4

Duffy says that the more we know about Christmas trees the more we'll sell.

Trish popped her finger out of her mouth and wiped it on the front of her jacket. "Gloves get in the way," she grumbled. "I don't see why I can't help with those trees with the soft needles." She pointed to the heap of Douglas firs I'd been propping against the fence.

Soft needles weren't the only reason she wanted to work on the firs. Mostly she wanted to be by ME. Ever since kindergarten, Trish has had a monster crush on me. She's not so bad really. It's just that I have no more interest in girls than I do in math. And I think math ought to be outlawed.

I looked at the huge number of trees and the long fence, and sighed again. "All right," I agreed. "You work on one end of the fence and I'll work on the other."

I didn't feel like talking. Not to her. Not to anybody. My best friend Zack Zeno was up inside the truck with Tony. They were moving the trees to the back of the truck bed while Luis, LaMar, and Sam Sherman wrestled the trees to the ground. I was the only boy stuck working on the lot with the cheerleaders. When you're the shortest guy on the team and the shortest person in the entire fourth grade, that's the kind of stuff that happens.

A beat-up yellow Honda crunched over the snow-packed lot and screeched to a stop. A woman and a little boy hopped out of the front seat.

"How much you askin' for the trees?" the woman called to Trish and me. She looked tired and scruffy like a lot of the people who live near Stan's Fresh Food Supermarket. Her long hair blew in front of her face. She fought the wind to yank it back.

"That depends on what kind you want, ma'am," I answered, flashing her a killer smile. Now that I had a customer, my bad mood lifted and flew off with the wind.

The woman frowned at the trees and looked around. "I want one with needles that won't fall off," she said. "Last year I got a tree that turned bald before Christmas even got here. We don't want any more bald trees, do we, Dewey?"

I looked down at the little kid hanging off her long, gray, puffy coat. His nose was running in a clear stream down to his top lip. "Nope," he said around the thumb in his mouth.

"You must have had a spruce," I said, trying to sound like an expert. "What you need is a nice Scotch pine." I ran over to a small heap of long-needled trees and grabbed a five-footer by the trunk. "This, ma'am, is America's favorite

Christmas tree." I felt like the guy who sells carpet on TV.

Trish did the freshness test while I twirled the tree, showing it off. The guy from the Christmas tree farm had taught us how to grab a branch and pull back on it. If it's a good tree you don't wind up with a handful of needles stuck to your glove when you let go. "See?" Trish asked, letting go of the branch. "This one's great. Nice and full too."

"How much?" the woman asked. I noticed she was missing a couple of front teeth.

I looked for the tag. "Thirteen dollars," I said, flashing her another big smile. I was beginning to think I was good at selling Christmas trees. Maybe not being on the truck would turn out to be fun.

The woman took a step back. "Thirteen dollars!" she gasped. "I can't afford $13 for a tree. What do you have for five or six?"

All our trees were prime-grade. None were smaller or cheaper than the one I was holding. The woman got back in the car. "Can't afford it," she mumbled.

We watched as she and Dewey drove off in a cloud of exhaust fumes. The wind whipped around the side of the market, bringing my bad mood back with it. "Well, we can't just stand here all day," I snapped at Trish. "Back to work!"

Trish glared at me again and stomped to the

other end of the fence. For a few minutes we worked quietly. I kept thinking about the woman in the yellow car. My family doesn't have a whole lot of money. My mom always says she pinches pennies so hard she makes Abraham Lincoln beg for mercy. But even so, I knew my dad had paid $13 for our tree last year. The lady in the yellow car had to be REALLY poor if she couldn't afford $13!

"Hey, Mick," Zack called. "How about a hot cocoa break?"

"Sure." I dropped the tree I'd just started to pick up. "Where's Coach?" I looked around the lot, but didn't see him.

"In the trailer," Zack replied. Sam Sherman's father had given us the use of a motor home while we sold trees. It gave us a place to warm up and also to take customers to write up their orders.

Mr. Sherman makes a ton of money as a lawyer in Cleveland. I used to think all that money was the reason his son Sam is such a creep, but I don't any more. Sam's brother Mike is rich too, but he would never call me "Shrimpo" or make fun of me like Sam does.

"On second thought, that's OK," I said. "We need to get these done."

The truth is, I didn't want to go in the trailer while Coach was there. I was still benched because of something that had happened at last week's game. I got jealous because Zack had been playing great and getting a lot of attention because his dad had left for Minnesota for four months. So I did a bunch of stupid stuff and ended up with one personal foul and one technical. The technical had turned Coach's face even redder than mine gets when I'm embarrassed. And, believe me, I'm a world-class blusher.

"Oh, yeah, I see what you mean," Zack said with a grin. He knew I wasn't on the best of terms with Coach these days. "I'm hungry. You think your mom's making fried chicken for supper?"

"Maybe," I answered. Zack is living at my house until his dad gets back from Minnesota. Mr. Zeno got laid off from the Ford plant until April. The only job he could get until then is one with the railroad. Since Zack doesn't have a mom at home, he either had to stay with us, or go to Chicago and live with an aunt and uncle he doesn't know.

"I'm going to see if one of the other guys wants to take a break," Zack said. "I'll catch up with you later, Mick," as he walked back toward the truck.

A woman with three little girls came out of the market. She stopped and gave each kid a coin to drop in the Salvation Army's red kettle. She smiled when she saw me watching.

"Hi!" I called. "Need a tree?"

"Not today!" she yelled back. "Thanks though!"

My heart sank. Stan's Fresh Food Supermarket sits right smack in the middle of three neighborhoods. The one where Sam Sherman lives has lots of big old mansion houses with towers and stained glass windows that rich people are fixing up. Trish's, Zack's, and my neighborhood has medium-sized old houses that are OK, but kind of plain. The third neighborhood has big old houses that have been cut up into tiny apartments. It's the kind of place where broken washing machines sit on the porch like furniture, and curtains flap out of the windows in the summer. Not many of the people who shop at Stan's Fresh Food Supermarket live in Sam's neighborhood.

A sudden racket crashed into my thoughts, sending them scattering like marbles. I let go of the tree I was propping and turned around. Over by the truck the team was huddled in a circle around something on the ground. Suddenly Zack broke away and ran toward the trailer.

"Mick!" he hollered when he saw me watching. "Get Coach! Tony fell off the truck!"

My heart thudded. For a second I just stood there staring. Then I broke into a sprint. At the motor home I took both steps at once and burst through the door, almost crashing head first into a cupboard. Coach was sitting at the table signing papers for the tree delivery. He looked up and started to frown until he saw my face.

"Tony fell off the truck!" I cried. I turned around and crashed into Zack. We jumped off the steps and raced back over to the truck with Coach pounding behind us.

Tony was down on the ground, clutching his shoulder. It was the same one he'd hurt last week when we played the Brunswick Blue Dolphins. The sound of his moans sent a shiver rippling through my insides.

Coach knelt down and unzipped Tony's jacket. He's not a doctor, but he's been a coach for a long time and has seen a lot of injuries. "I don't think it's broken," he said when he was done looking. "But you're not going to be playing much ball with this," he told Tony.

My heart speeded up. I was sixth man on the team. If Tony was out, that could only mean one thing. I was the new starter for the Pinecrest Flying Eagles!

2

A Very Shaky Start

"Don't say anything about it, OK?" I begged Zack on the way home from the tree lot. "Coach might still be so mad at me from Saturday he won't let me have Tony's spot." That thought had wriggled its way into my brain and refused to go away.

"It has to be you, Mick. Who else could it be? Nobody else is even half as good as you are," Zack insisted. "I think you're worried for nothing. You're in!"

He slapped me a high five and I slapped it back. But I wasn't so sure. There was a time, not long ago, when I'd had it in the bag. Coach had even told me I could take Zack's place when he went to Chicago. But he hadn't gone and now things were different. I'd poked a guy in the ribs with my elbow to keep him from making a shot, and Coach had called it cheating. The word still knotted my stomach like a pretzel.

The next night at practice Coach Duffy shrilled his whistle as soon as we got out on the floor.

"OK, guys, listen up!" he hollered. "We've got no time for fooling around here. We've got a game Saturday and one of our best men is down. I talked with Tony's mother this morning and she says he's out for the rest of the season."

I felt like a paper airplane at the point of take-off—would I soar or stay grounded? I looked at Zack. He flashed me a grin and gave me the OK sign down low where Coach wouldn't see it. The plane headed upward.

Coach Duffy cleared his throat and looked around. "Normally," he began, "Tony's spot would be filled by the sixth man ..."

The paper airplane that was me took a hard nosedive. He'd said "normally." This must not be normal time. I stared at the floor and tried to keep the hot red stain burning my chest from creeping up my neck.

"But we had a problem last week that makes that impossible," Coach continued.

The red stain bled all over my face. I felt like I'd been dipped in beet juice.

"Nick, it looks like you'll start on Saturday," he said to Nick Clemmons. "After that, we'll have to see how it goes. OK, that's it. Let's go! Laps!"

I fell into place behind Zack. My legs pumped up and down, but I don't know how I kept running around the gym. All I could hear was

Coach's voice in my head telling Nick he could start.

Saturday morning I woke up wishing it were a school day. I didn't dare come down with anything though. Even if I got black swamp fever or malaria, I'd have to show up. If I skipped a game Coach would call it being a bad sport—maybe even as bad as poking a guy in the ribs. We were playing the Wadsworth Wildcats. From what I'd heard, my quickness was just what we needed to win. But all I would be doing for the whole game was sitting on the bench—watching.

The teams lined up. The ball went up in the air and Sam Sherman claimed it. Right away the Wildcats spread out like a picnic blanket, forcing Sam to pass to Luis. It was a bad move. Luis panicked. He looked around, found himself smack in the middle of a Wildcat convention, and shot from too far out. The ball hit the rim and bounced. The Wildcat's center, a big lug of a kid with buzzed hair, sprinted in for the grab and sank it.

I gritted my teeth and closed my eyes as both teams tore across the court. I could hardly bear to watch. When I opened them again I had to blink to believe it. The Wildcats had slowed down and were passing the ball like it was a game of Hot Potato! Our guys darted and danced. But it was no use. The Wildcat's center lunged in for another jump shot and nailed it.

Trish Riley flew up off the floor. "Let's go, Pinecrest!" she hollered, jabbing the air with her fist. The rest of the cheerleaders jumped up and jabbed too. "Let's go, Pinecrest!" they agreed. "Let's GO!"

The only place Pinecrest went was down the tubes. By half time we were nine points short. There wasn't enough room in the gym to hold my energy. I felt like my skin would crack and a bolt of pure fire would break out and burn through the center of the game like lightning. I wanted out there so bad my muscles twitched.

"Coach, please put Mickey in!" LaMar pleaded in the locker room at half-time. "We're in trouble out there."

"Please, Coach," Zack agreed. "We need him to break up that ball-pass thing they keep doing."

Coach didn't look at me. He just shook his head no.

"But why?" Luis pushed. "He knows not to get another technical. We really, really need him! Please, Coach!"

Coach Duffy's thick neck turned back and forth. No. No. And no. "Mickey could be a big help," he agreed. "But it's not gonna happen. Sportsmanship is more important than a win.

Now back out on the floor! Remember, their biggest advantage is their man-to-man defense. You gotta be faster, Clemmons."

Defense is exactly why I would be so good out there. I may be short, but I'm so fast it's like I have eight legs. That's why the local newspaper calls me "Spider" McGhee. But it was clear that Coach would rather take a thumping from the Wildcats than let me spin a web.

We ended the fourth quarter down 17 points. The mood in the locker room after the game was quiet and glum. Even Sam Sherman didn't hit me with a volley of insults. I changed fast and went out to join my family. I hadn't wanted them to come since I wouldn't be playing. But Dad said a real fan supports the team no matter what.

"Sorry, buddy," he said, smoothing down the stick-up hair on top of my head. "You guys gave it all you had."

I didn't answer. I hadn't given it anything.

"I saved you part of my hot dog, Mickey," my little sister Meggie said. She stuck out a soggy squished piece of sandwich. It oozed catsup like blood from a cut.

"Uh, that's nice, Meg," I muttered. "Thanks, but I'm not hungry."

"Try not to feel too bad, honey," Mom comforted me. "You'll be back in the game next week."

Maybe so, but the big question is, would I be back as a starter? We headed over to the doors to wait for Zack. I stared at the speckled floor tiles and didn't say anything.

"Mickey!"

I cringed. Coach Duffy was heading toward us, his silver whistle swaying like a necklace. "May I talk to you please?" He nodded at my parents and said, "I need to borrow your son for half a second."

Mutely, I followed him over by the locker room door. He wanted one of two things. To tell me my next shift at the Christmas tree lot, or to lecture me about the technical again. I waited for him to say something. My throat felt tight, like somebody had me in a choke-hold.

"The guys think I've been too tough on you," Coach began.

He looked at me hard, right in the eye. I shifted my feet and tried to look back. I met his gaze, looked away, and looked back again.

"You probably think the same thing," he added.

I didn't know what I thought. On the one hand, I knew what I'd done was wrong. It made me feel like a worm every time I thought about it. But on the other hand, it wasn't like I'm the kind of guy who usually does things like that. I'm a team player. Anybody who knows me would say that.

"I know I've been firm about this," Coach continued, still looking me square in the eye. "But I am not going to be known as a coach who doesn't care about the rules or only wants to win. You're a good kid, Mickey. You know it and I know it. But I had to make an example of you, so nobody else would get the idea that it's OK to be a wise guy. Understand?"

I nodded. That part I understood fine. What I *didn't* understand is where it left me.

Coach grinned. "Christmas is coming," he said, "and I've got the holiday spirit. So I'm going to let you start next week. Do a good job and we'll keep it that way the rest of the season. Deal?"

It was like somebody had flipped on a light switch in my head. I could feel the beam shining through my eyes, turning them brighter than Christmas tree bulbs. Not those little, puny white ones either, but the big jumbo kind Dad uses to trim the porch.

"Deal," I said.

Coach Duffy ruffled my hair and grinned. "All right then, go on. I told your family I'd only borrow you for half a second. But remember, I said 'we'll see.' "

I ran back to the door. Zack had joined Mom,

Dad, and Meggie. I was smiling so hard I thought my face would break. "Guess what?" I announced. "I'm a starter!"

"Mickey!" Mom and Dad cried, grabbing me for a family hug. Mom reached out and pulled Zack in too. Meggie scrunched inside the huddle. She grabbed the knee of my jeans with one hand and the knee of Zack's with the other. When we finally came up for air, her hair stuck out all over her head from static electricity. She looked like a baby Einstein.

Mom tried to smooth Meggie's hair down, but it crackled and stood on end again. We all laughed. It would have been the perfect beginning to the perfect Christmas. If hadn't been for those two scary little words: "*We'll see.*"

3

What Do You Think These Trees Are For?

A spicy blast of hot tomatoes, cheese, pepperoni, and green peppers filled the kitchen as Mom pulled a homemade pizza from the oven. She cut a slice, put it on a plate, and handed it to Zack. Swallowing hard, I watched her run the round cutter through the rest. I was so hungry I could eat the whole thing.

"Oh, guys, I almost forgot," she said as she picked up a slice for me. A long, gooey string of hot cheese stretched out a foot. "I was over at the church today and my mission circle decided on the most wonderful Christmas project. You're going to love it!"

"Huh?" I took the plate, but didn't start eating.

Mom laughed and lifted a slice of pizza for Meggie. "I know, I know. You're busy," she said before I could say it myself. "But this is really great. It won't take up too much time and you guys will have a ball with it."

I seriously doubted it. Between Christmas trees

and basketball, I didn't have time for one more thing. I grabbed my pizza and bit off the point. "Owwwwwwwww!" I howled as hot cheese had plastered itself to the roof of my mouth.

Mom handed me a glass of cold milk. "Slow down," she warned. "Pizza doesn't have legs. It's not going anywhere. Now the thing is, we're going to try and form a doggie parade and visit the nursing home for the holidays."

The pain in my mouth numbed. "Oh, Mom, noooooooooo!" I cried. "I don't wanna do that! There's no time and … and …" I looked at Zack for help. He hunched over his plate and wouldn't look at me. "I have to work a lot harder if I want to keep being a starter," I continued, talking fast. "Besides, I'd feel weird going in a place like that."

Mom's eyes widened. "Mickey! I can't believe what I'm hearing. Old people are nothing to be afraid of," she said. "Grandma McGhee is old and you aren't afraid of her."

Grandma McGhee wears funny aprons with strings that fly out behind her. She makes lopsided cakes with icing so hard it crunches when you cut it. Sometimes she gives me dollar bills when no one is looking. But that's different. Grandma McGhee is MY old person. I wouldn't know any of *those* old people.

"I'm not scared exactly," I said. "I just don't

want to do it." I didn't know if that was true or not. About not being scared, I mean. The truth is, even Grandma McGhee scares me sometimes. When she takes out her false teeth, her mouth caves in and she doesn't look like my grandma anymore.

Mom finished slicing the pizza and handed a plate to Meggie. "Well, I don't think it's a choice this time," she said finally. "We need dogs that are good with people. And Muggsy and Piston fill the bill." She looked at Zack. Muggsy is my dog and Piston is his. "I want you guys to ask Trish too," she told him. "And Dulcie can bring Taco."

Dulcie is a little kid who just moved in across the street. A couple weeks ago, when I was trying to get money to go see the Harlem Globetrotters, I'd started a babysitting business. Dulcie was the kid I babysat. As mad as I felt, I had to smile at the thought of Dulcie storming the nursing home with her skinny, hairless dog Taco. That would sure wake those old people up! Dulcie only has two volumes—loud and louder.

After lunch I wandered across the street to ask her about the doggie parade.

"Oh, that's so GOOD, Mickey!" Dulcie squealed, hopping around the living room. "Taco would love to see all the grandmas and grandpas. Wouldn't you, Taco?" She stopped jumping long enough to plant a noisy kiss on her dog's wet, black nose. Then she said in a serious voice, "My grandpa's in heaven, you know."

"Uh, that's too bad. I mean, that's good," I mumbled, zipping my jacket. I didn't know what I meant. I just knew I didn't want to talk about old people anymore. "Mom says you can dress Taco up for Christmas if you want to."

Dulcie ignored me "My Grandpa loooooooves heaven. Sometimes he even winks at me from up there," she said.

"Huh?" I stopped trying to fit the pointed end of my zipper into its socket and looked at her. "He can't do that." But even as I said it, I was already sorry. In less than a second I knew I would be needing ear plugs.

"DON'T YOU SAY THAT TO ME!" Dulcie screamed, stomping her foot. "HE CAN TOO WINK, BECAUSE I SAW HIM! YOU'RE BEING A BAD NEIGHBOR!"

She used to call me a bad babysitter. "OK," I said. "I'm sorry. Whatever. But you'll join the parade, right?"

"Right," Dulcie said in a normal voice.

I started to go home, then changed my mind, and walked up the street to Trish's house. I told her about the nursing home project and asked if she wanted to bring her dog, Gabrielle. Gabrielle is sort of a dumb dog name, but she's Muggsy's and Piston's little sister. We found all three puppies in the church parking lot a couple of months ago.

"Sure, that would be great, Mickey," Trish agreed. "Want to come in?"

I shuffled from one foot to the other and stomped the snow off my boots. "Uh, thanks, but I can't," I mumbled. "Today's my day at the tree lot."

"Mine too!" she squealed. "I'll see you there then."

Zack and I got to the tree lot early. Because of the game, parents had had to take over the first shift by themselves. You could sure tell they were glad to see us. They were stomping their feet and blowing on their fingers in the cold.

"Business has been slow," a mom with a muffler over her mouth reported. She shivered and held her steaming coffee up by her nose. "We only sold two. Both small."

I sighed. If things didn't pick up pretty soon, we'd never get our new uniforms. I was beginning to wish we'd gone with the candy idea. Everybody likes candy, especially during the holidays. And candy costs a lot less than trees.

When the parents left, Zack and I walked around the lot propping up the trees that had fallen over. As soon as Trish and her friend Brittany showed up, we told them about the slow sales.

"The problem is we're just standing around waiting for people to come to us," Trish complained. "We need to get out there and grab their attention."

I didn't say so, but that's exactly what I'd done last time. And it hadn't worked. An old lady in a red coat and short boots ringed with fur was walking slowly across the lot toward us. Trish gave me a little push. "Go get her, Mickey!" she whispered.

The idea of giving old ladies the hard sell made me wince. But I walked over to meet her. "Hi," I said brightly. "May I help you with something today?"

She looked at the price tag on a small Douglas fir and balked. "Eighteen dollars! That's highway robbery! I'm on Social Security. I can't pay these kind of prices."

I swallowed hard. All I know about Social Security is that Grandma McGhee lives on it too. She waits for it to come every month like I wait for Christmas. "I have a Scotch pine for $13," I offered weakly.

The old woman shook her head. "Too much," she snapped. "I'm not made of money, sonny." If she realized she'd made a rhyme, she didn't act like it. She walked away muttering about what the world had come to.

It was the same old story over and over. Nobody could afford our trees. When she was gone, I flopped into a folding chair one of the parents had placed by the fence. "This is baaaaaaaaaad!" I moaned. "We should have sold our trees somewhere else."

"We couldn't," Zack reminded me. "This was the only store that would let us."

Trish and Brittany nodded agreement. For a second we stared at the line of cars going in and out of the market. Then Trish smacked her forehead and let out a squeal.

"Wait! I've got it! It's so simple, I can't believe we never thought of it before!" she cried.

I waited for her to announce her bright idea, but she grabbed Brittany's arm and pulled her over by the motor home. Zack and I watched as they talked and giggled.

"What do you suppose that's all about?" Zack asked.

"Beats me," I said, standing back up. I wondered if we should rearrange the trees.

The girls walked past us and lined up next to each other near the edge of the lot by the street.

"READY?" Brittany hollered.

"OK!" Trish answered.

ONE! TWO! THREE! FOUR!
WHAT DO YOU THINK THESE TREES
ARE FOR?

The girls led the cheer, lunging to the right and yanking the horn of an imaginary truck.

TO TRIM 'EM! TO TRIM 'EM!
YEAH, YEAH, TO TRIM 'EM!

Brittany jumped with both legs stretched in an upside-down "V." Trish did one of those weird jumps that doesn't even look possible. She stuck both legs out in front so straight she looked like she was sitting. And then—faster than you can say "Oh Little Town of Bethlehem"—she WAS sitting. Right in the big pile of snow left by the snowplow!

A pickup truck slowed to a stop. The driver, a young guy with a scraggly beard, laughed so hard he pounded on his steering wheel with his fist.

Trish scrambled up out of the snowbank. "ONE! TWO! THREE! FOUR!" she chanted.

The driver rolled down his window and stuck out his head. "WATCH HOW FAST I HIT THE FLOOR!" he chanted back. He gunned his engine and roared down Wooster Street.

4

Dulcie and the Coyote Call

A creepy feeling came over me as we pulled into the parking lot of the nursing home. I'd been past the two brick buildings a million times, but I'd never been inside.

"We'll be going to the assisted living part," Mom explained to me, Zack, Meggie, and Dulcie. "The people who live in that building only need a little help. Some of them even drive their own cars."

I felt a small swell of hope. "What are we supposed to do exactly?" I asked, snapping Muggsy's red leash on his collar. Dulcie slipped a small green wreath with a red bow around Taco's skinny, hairless neck. Trish was planning to get a Santa suit for Gabrielle. Only Zack and I had decided that our dogs were cheerful enough plain.

"I talked to the activities lady," Mom replied as she helped Dulcie with Taco's leash. "She said the best thing is to make a parade of dogs and walk up and down the halls. Then, when everyone's seen them, we can split up and visit."

Visiting is what I'd been afraid of. I guess I didn't mind parading around, but I sure didn't want to have to sit and talk with just one person. What would I talk about? Christmas trees? Basketball? Old people wouldn't be interested in stuff like that.

A short woman with a loud laugh and a cheerful voice met us at the door. "I'm Mrs. Wilkins, the activities director," she said. "Welcome to Meadowview."

I looked around. Through the windows I could see the busy street, the parking lot, and a patio that overlooked a brick storage building. There wasn't a single meadow in sight. To the right, a couple of old people watched a movie on a big screen TV. A huge Christmas tree packed with ornaments stood in one corner. A brick fireplace took up another. The whole place smelled like medicine, pine cleaner, and cooked spinach.

"We're waiting for two more," Mom told Mrs. Wilkins. "I'm sure they'll be here any second. "There are four others coming on Friday."

Just then the door opened behind us and Trish and Brittany hurried in with their dogs. Gabrielle looked silly in her Santa hat. I hate it when people dress up dogs. Brittany's dog, a huge German shepherd, strained at its leash and barked.

Mrs. Wilkins frowned. "I don't know about

that one," she said of the shepherd.

"Oh, he'll be OK," Brittany assured her. "Silver Boy's just excited."

If Silver Boy got any more excited, all that would be left of him would be a heap of fur on the floor. Mrs. Wilkins shook her head. "I want him at the very back of the parade. If he doesn't settle down, he'll have to go back outside," she warned.

Brittany sighed and stood back as we formed a line. Trish tugged on her baseball cap and smiled at me. "Do you mind if I go first, Mickey?" she asked.

"I don't care," I mumbled. I motioned to Zack to get in line behind her. Muggsy and I got behind Zack and Piston, and Dulcie and Taco got behind me. Brittany yanked Silver Boy to the end.

"OK, everybody ready?" Mrs. Wilkins asked when we finally formed a crooked parade. "This is going to be fun!"

She led us down a long hallway lined with doors. A few were closed, but most were open at least partway. As soon as they saw the dogs, old people filled the hall. A few used metal walkers or leaned on canes.

"Oh, what a little darling!" a lady with a head full of pink curlers squealed at Taco. She tried to pet him, but Dulcie had to pick Taco up for her.

"Why don't we sing 'Jingle Bells'?" Mom suggested. She was walking beside us, trying to help Brittany control Silver Boy.

Dulcie didn't wait to be asked twice. "JINGLE BELLS! JINGLE BELLS!" she screeched before anyone else could begin. She hit a note so flat you could have driven a truck over it.

At the back of the line, Silver Boy's ears twitched. He shook his head, stepped sideways, and let out a howl like a coyote.

Dulcie stopped singing and whirled around. "BE QUIET, YOU BAD DOG!" she yelled.

Silver Boy barked. Dulcie glared at him and picked up her song.

Silver Boy threw back his head and howled louder.

Dulcie stopped singing and stomped over to him. She was so small she met him eyeball to eyeball. "Listen, you bad old dog, " she shouted. "I'M the singer and YOU'RE the walker. Got that?"

The old people roared. Dulcie grinned at them and picked up her song one more time. Silver Boy howled again.

"OK, THAT'S IT! I'M GETTING MAD NOW!" Dulcie tossed her fuzzy hair, hiked up her skirt, and stalked to the end of the line.

I laughed so hard I dropped Muggsy's leash and fell against the wall, holding my sides. Dulcie wagged her finger at Silver Boy's nose. "If you knew how to sing, it would be different," she told him sternly. "But you are A BAD SINGER."

Suddenly Mom darted past me. "Mickey! Get him!" she shouted.

I looked around. For a second I didn't know what she was talking about. Then I saw my dog fly around the corner of the hall so fast it looked like all four paws were off the ground.

"Muggggseeeee!" I called, dashing after Mom.

The activities lady came out of a room and hurried after us in her red high heels. Mom and I beat her by a mile. We stood in a new hall and looked around.

"He must have gone into a room," Mom said. "You take this side and I'll take that one." She knocked on a half-open door and stuck her head in.

Behind us I could hear Brittany, Zack, and Dulcie still trying to sing "Jingle Bells." I felt weird knocking on strange bedroom doors. Mrs. Wilkins came up behind me. "Stay calm," she told me. "It's OK."

We went to four more rooms. Muggsy wasn't in any of them. I dashed ahead to the fifth, leaving Mrs. Wilkins talking to a guy who wanted to know the dinner menu. Before I could knock, an old man looked up and smiled. He was sitting in an overstuffed, blue chair watching TV. A dog lay draped across his lap. It looked like it had been made on Friday with a week's worth of leftover dog parts.

"This what you lookin' for?" the man asked with a slow, easy smile. He pointed down to Muggsy who opened one eye and looked at me.

"I'm sorry, sir," I said, quickly. "I'll take him away."

"Oh, no," the old man said. "He's fine. You come in and sit a spell. I haven't had any company since … I can't remember when."

I stood in the doorway and looked back down the hall. "I got him, Mom!" I called. Mom faked a huge relief scene which made me laugh. I was still smiling when I turned back to the man.

"Hi," I said, uncertainly. "I'm Mickey McGhee. That's Muggsy in your lap."

The man scratched Muggsy's ears and smiled up at me again. Something about him made my feet go forward into the room. "Hello there, Mickey McGhee," he greeted me. "I'm pleased to meet you. You can call me Tom."

There was nowhere to sit, so I perched nervously on the edge of the bed and looked around. The room was very clean. Besides the bed and the blue chair, there was a TV on a stand, an old-fashioned radio as big as a tank, and a china closet filled with pink flowered dishes. The old man followed my gaze to the dishes.

"Belonged to my wife," he explained. "That woman sure loved her wedding china! Couldn't bring myself to part with it when she passed. So here I am, an old man with a lot of fancy dishes." He chuckled and scratched Muggsy's ears again.

For a second, nobody said anything. I could feel myself start to relax. "So, what you been up to, Mickey McGhee?" Tom asked finally.

"Selling Christmas trees mostly," I told him.

"I don't have much use for Christmas trees these days," Tom replied. "But I do know a thing or two about sellin', I reckon." He looked over at the doorway and smiled. "Well, well, who might you be, little lady?"

I turned around. Dulcie was standing in the doorway, hanging onto Taco's leash. "Dulcie Ann Steffins," she announced, bouncing into the room. Dulcie stopped in front of Tom's chair and looked him over. "I like your hair," she announced. "It's just like mine."

Tom laughed and ran a wrinkled hand over the top of his thick, white hair. "Thank you," he told her. "You got you some pretty good hair too, Miss Dulcie."

Dulcie's hair is many things, but good will never be one of them. It's the fuzziest hair I've ever seen growing out of a human head. I laughed right out loud.

Dulcie glared at me and smiled at Tom. "Thank you," she replied. "You're a GOOD old grandpa. I like you."

I felt my face turn pink as a party dress. Leave it to Dulcie to call an old person old right to his face. But I had to agree with her. Tom was a good guy. I liked him too.

The phone next to the bed shrilled. I jumped and looked over at it.

"Get that for me, will you, Mickey?" Tom asked. He leaned forward and lowered the volume on the TV.

I reached for the receiver, but I didn't pick it up. Next to the phone, a young African-American man in a weird, old-time basketball uniform grinned at me from a silver frame. I picked up the picture. It was an old, yellowed basketball card. On the bottom it said Tom "Stringbean" Jackson, Cleveland Rosenblum Celtics.

5

A Thing or Two
about Sellin'

I stared at the picture, then at Tom, then back at the picture. I forgot all about the ringing phone.

Dulcie scrambled over and picked it up. "Hello," she said into the receiver. There were a few seconds of silence. Then she said, "I'm Dulcie Ann Steffins. Me and Taco and Mickey and Muggsy are visiting this grandpa."

"Is that you?" I asked Tom, pointing at the basketball card.

The old man nodded. "Oh lands! That was a long, long time ago. Back in '27."

My eyes popped. "You mean 1927?"

"OK," Dulcie said into the phone. "I'll tell him. Bye."

Dulcie turned to Tom. "That was your daughter, Hairy Etta. She said she'll call you later." She walked over to Tom's blue chair and perched on the edge next to Muggsy's tail.

"How old were you in this picture?" I asked.

"Oh my. Let me see." Tom's wrinkled forehead

formed deep grooves. "I'm 92 now and that was … I reckon I was 20."

"Wow," I breathed. "You played pro ball, huh?" I went back over and sat on the bed.

Dulcie let out a huge sigh, and slumped back against Tom before he could answer. "Oh, pooooooooooooooooor Hairy Etta!" she moaned.

"Huh?" I stopped looking at the card and stared at Dulcie. "What are you talking about?" I asked.

"Hairy Etta," she repeated patiently. She rolled her eyes back and looked at Tom upside down. "That's a BAD name for a girl, you know."

Red spots bloomed on my cheeks like twin roses. "I'm sorry," I said quickly. "She didn't mean …"

But Tom was rocking back and forth in his chair. "My daughter's name is Harrietta," he said when he stopped laughing. "That's only one word. She's named after my mother. You remind me of her when she was your age, Miss Dulcie. You surely do."

Relief poured over me like a warm shower. Tom had a sense of humor. "Did you play pro?" I asked him again. I didn't want to give Dulcie a chance to say anything else.

Tom nodded. "As pro as it was in those days. It wasn't like it is today. No sir! No NBA back then.

Just the American Basketball League in '25. Still, we packed 'em in at Public Hall. First game back in '23, they made a double header. One game in the afternoon and one game in the evenin'. They sure don't do that these days. 27,000 people came downtown to watch. Mmmmm-mmmmm, that was really somethin'!"

"I play basketball," I said shyly. "I just made starter."

Tom leaned forward in his chair and studied me. I knew what he was thinking—that I'm too small for basketball. But he surprised me. "I'll bet you're a point guard, like that Earl Boykins of the Cavaliers," he said. He chuckled and scratched Muggsy's ears. "I sure do like watchin' that Earl Boykins. Sure hope they sign him up for good. You serious about the game?"

I nodded. "I plan to be in the NBA. People say I can't, but I don't believe it."

Tom nodded his approval. "Good for you!" he said. "That kind of can't-do talk is only for the foolish. You get yourself right with God, and there isn't anythin' you can't do, I reckon. 'But seek first His kingdom and His righteousness, and all these things will be given to you as well.' It says that right in the Good Book. Matthew 6:33. You know about that?" he asked.

"Yes! And I believe it too!" I cried, jumping off

the bed. "There's this one guy, Sam Sherman. He always makes fun of me, but I went out for the team and I made it. The newspaper calls me Spider McGhee because ..." I was talking so fast the words were tripping over themselves.

Mom popped her head in the door. "Oh, there you are!" she cried when she saw me. " Talking a mile a minute" She turned to Tom. "I hope my son's not wearing you out."

"No, ma'am," Tom answered. He winked at me. "I reckon we're a couple o' kindred spirits, me and this boy."

I couldn't believe my ears. He meant we were just alike! A professional basketball player thought I was just like him! All the way home in the car I couldn't stop chattering about Tom Jackson and the Cleveland Rosenblum Celtics.

The next night at practice, Coach announced that I would start in Saturday's game. I glanced over at Nick Clemmons. He stared at the floor. A muscle next to his mouth twitched. Nick's a good guy, but he really isn't as good a player as I am. That's not bragging. It's the simple truth. But I still felt bad for him. It hurts to want something that bad and not get it.

"OK, now that that's out of the way," Coach continued when everyone was done high-fiving me, "we need to talk about tree sales."

The whole team groaned. By now everyone had worked a shift and knew that our chances of getting uniforms were fading fast. In almost a week, we had only sold six trees.

"I think I know what's causing our problem," Coach said. "There's a lot three blocks west on Wooster that has cut-rate prices. Poor quality trees, but cheap."

"So what are we supposed to do?" LaMar wailed. "We can't sell ours for any less, can we? We have to pay the tree farm guy and have room for a profit."

"That's right," Coach agreed. "I think we need to be more creative."

The team exchanged glances. Nobody had a single idea how to be creative.

"Well, you boys think about it," Coach Duffy said. "If anybody has any ideas, let me know. All right then, let's go! Sherman, what's with the two different shoes?"

All eyes turned to Sam Sherman. He was wearing a black basketball shoe on his right foot, and a white one on his left. "I'm starting a trend," he said like he was cool.

"Not on my team you're not," Coach barked. "Change one of those shoes or sit on the bench."

Sam slunk off to the locker room, scowling. I didn't bother to enjoy it. I was too excited to be a starter and too busy trying to think of what to do about our Christmas tree problem. Halfway through warm-up jumping jacks, I had a brain flash. Tom Jackson at the nursing home had said, "I know a thing or two about sellin', I reckon." Maybe he could help us figure out how to sell more trees.

After practice I cornered Zack in the locker room. "Will you come to the nursing home with me? I want to talk to Tom about our tree problem. You'll get to meet him. He's really great."

Zack unzipped his gym bag. I could tell he was thinking it over. He hadn't had as good a time at Meadowview as I'd had. A lady who made dolls out of dishwashing soap bottles had spent the whole visit showing him stiff plastic figures wearing dresses that felt like sponge.

"Oh, come on," I urged him. "You'll like Tom. I promise."

"All right," Zack agreed. But I could tell he really didn't want to.

Before he could change his mind, I ran to the phone and called Mom. She said OK as long as we called her for a ride when we were done. Zack and I walked fast in the cold and got to the nursing home right before they started serving dinner. The halls smelled good this time, like roast chicken and mashed potatoes. We checked in at the desk and went straight to Tom's room.

"Well, look here!" Tom cried when he saw me at the door. His face glowed with pleasure. "What are you doin' back here so soon, young fella?"

"Hi, Tom," I greeted him. "This is my friend, Zack Zeno."

I waited while they shook hands, then got right to our tree problem. "Tom, we need some advice," I said after telling him the story. "You said you know something about selling. Do you know anything about a problem like ours?"

Tom folded his hands, making a little steeple of his two pointer fingers. He rested his chin on them and considered the question. "As a matter of fact I do," he said after a few seconds. "Remember yesterday when we were talkin' basketball and I told you about the Rosenblum Celtics? That's a strange name, Rosenblum Celtics, don't you agree?"

I nodded, wishing he would get to the point. As much as I wanted to talk basketball, right now I had to get some answers about selling Christmas trees.

"Well," Tom continued, motioning us to sit on the bed. "Our team was owned by a man named Max Rosenblum. He owned a clothing store in Cleveland and he had a pretty good slogan—'It's easy to pay the Rosenblum way.' "

Zack and I looked at each other. "What was the

Rosenblum way?" Zack asked.

Tom chuckled. "Well, I can't say as I remember for sure," he admitted. "But Mr. Rosenblum let people have credit. That was back before they had plastic credit cards like nowadays. Seems to me you could let people pick a tree and pay a little at a time 'til Christmas. You could mark their name on the tree and then, when they are paid up, they could take it home."

I thought about that. "But they could buy a tree cheap at the other place," I reminded him. "And take it home right away."

Tom nodded. "True enough," he agreed. "That's why you need yourselves an angle. Looks to me like you got one built in. It's right there plain as puddin'. You tell them the truth—that it's danger-ous havin' a tree that's not fresh. Tell them they'd be riskin' fire. When old houses catch fire, they burn up faster than you can say 'Jimminy Cricket!' "

Zack and I looked at each other again. "It's easy to pay the Pinecrest way!" we cried, slapping each other a high five. Both of us high-fived Tom. He smiled so wide we could see a gold tooth shining way back in his mouth.

"Thanks, Tom!" I cried. "You're a life saver!"

Tom grinned. "I don't know about that," he said, "but I reckon I know a thing or two about sellin'."

6

A New Shade of Red

"So what do you think?" I asked Coach Duffy after Zack and I explained Tom's tree idea.

Coach frowned. "Not bad. Except for one thing. Christmas is only two weeks away. How are folks going to afford a tree in two weeks if they can't afford one now? That's not a whole lot of time to pay it off."

Zack and I exchanged glances. We hadn't thought about that.

"I do like the safety angle though," Coach said when we didn't reply. Suddenly he threw his arms up in the air. "Oh, let's try it! What have we got to lose?"

Trish, Zack, and I made two huge banners. One said IT'S EASY TO PAY THE PINECREST WAY! The other said FRESH TREES ARE SAFE TREES. Just as we were putting the lid on the green poster paint, Zack jumped up off the floor.

"Hey! I have an idea!" he cried. "Trish, your cheerleading the other day is what made me think of it. How about if you come up with a catchy cheer that tells people what we mean? We could clear off a spot and melt the ice, so you wouldn't fall this time."

I grinned at Trish. "You wouldn't get cold if you were jumping around," I reminded her.

But Trish didn't need convincing. Already she was muttering cheers under her breath and jabbing the air.

The next day Zack and I showed up on the lot with the signs. Stan, the owner of the market, let us tack the signs to the front of the fence. By the time Trish got there, they were already in place. People were even slowing down to read them.

"Wait 'til you hear the cheer Brittany and I came up with!" she cried, running over to the spot Zack had shoveled and sprinkled with rock salt. Trish turned her back to the street, and brought both green and white pompons up to her chest. Then she spread her arms out wide and yelled:

APPLES, PINECONES, PUMPKIN PIE!
BUY FROM US, WE'LL TELL YOU WHY!

ALL OUR TREES ARE FRESH AS RAIN!
DON'T THROW MONEY DOWN THE
   DRAIN!

DON'T RISK DANGER, DON'T RISK
    SMOKE!

A BURNING HOUSE IS NOT A JOKE!
SHORT ON CASH? THAT'S OK!
YOU CAN PAY THE PINECREST WAY!

Trish ended with a huge leap, then dropped to the ground on one knee. "What do you think?" she asked.

Zack and I looked at each other and shrugged. What we knew about cheerleading would fit in a bottle cap with room left over.

"Sounds good," I said. At least it was lively.

"Isn't it a little—uh—long?" Zack asked.

"It has to be long to get everything in," Trish answered. She tugged on her bright red baseball cap and smiled at me. A big hunk of plastic holly dangled off the side. "Mickey likes it, don't you, Mickey?" she asked.

I was saved from having to answer. Brittany's mom dropped her off and the two girls turned toward the street and started cheering. Cars honked and people coming out of the market stopped to listen. But nobody bought any trees.

"I don't get it," Zack said after half an hour. "It's not working."

I didn't get it either. Offering credit was such a

great idea. It had worked for that Rosenblum guy. It had worked for lots of people. Why didn't it work for us?

"Hey, look," Zack said suddenly.

A long, shiny black car was gliding slowly through the entrance to the market. Its driver, an older man wearing dark sunglasses, took his time scanning the lot. First he looked at the trees. Then he looked at us. It was kind of creepy being stared at by somebody whose eyes you couldn't see.

Finally, the man swung into a parking space and stopped the car. We watched as he took off the glasses and stashed them on the dashboard. I held my breath as he got out of the car, praying he wouldn't head for the market.

"He's coming over!" Zack whispered.

The man nodded to us as he trudged over to our biggest, most expensive spruces. He folded his arms and stared at them. He wasn't the sort of person who usually shopped at Stan's Fresh Food Supermarket. He was dressed all in black and wore a black hat pulled down over his eyebrows. In the bright sunlight, his black shoes were so shiny they looked like they were glazed with ice. There was something sort of spooky about him. I shifted uneasily from one foot to the other.

"Should we go over, or let him look by himself for awhile?" I whispered to Zack.

"Go over," Zack whispered back.

Neither of us moved.

"Go on," Zack hissed, giving me a little shove. "Go ON!"

I wanted to ask why he didn't go over himself if he was so eager. But there wasn't time. The man was watching me from under the brim of the menacing black hat. I took a deep breath and pasted on a friendly smile.

"Hi!" I called. "Anything I can help you with?"

"Maybe," the strange man said. With his black leather glove, he tugged at a branch. "How much you asking for the 12-footers?" His voice was deep and low with a froggy sound to it. The hair on my arms stood up.

"Th-th-thirty-five dollars," I stammered. Was it my imagination or had his eyes flickered to the motor home where we kept the cash box?

The man nodded. "Hmmmm," he said, fingering another branch.

Out by the street Trish and Brittany saw we had a customer and headed over. I wildly shook my head no, but they kept right on coming. The last thing we needed was everybody rushing this guy. I had no idea who—or what—he was. But one thing was for sure—he was no ordinary customer.

I shook my head harder at the girls. The man stopped looking at the trees and swung around to see why I was acting weird. An icy ghost breath shivered down my spine as his glittering blue eyes met mine.

Trish and Brittany rattled their pompons and spread their arms. "APPLES, PINECONES, PUMPKIN PIE! BUY OUR TREES WE'LL TELL YOU WHY!"

The man in the black coat turned back to watch the cheer. Desperately, I slashed my finger across my throat. "Cut! Cut!" I tried to tell them. Neither of them noticed.

"DON'T RISK DANGER, DON'T RISK SMOKE!" the girls cried, kicking their legs over their heads.

The man unbuttoned his coat and reached into an inside pocket. The quick motion backed me up so fast I nearly crashed into a tree.

"A BURNING HOUSE IS NOT A JOKE!" the cheer continued.

I looked at Zack, but he was watching the girls. Images of movie bad guys flooded my brain.

Black clothes.

Cold, steely eyes.

Low, froggy voices.

Few words.

Big, black cars.

Another ghost breath rippled down my spine. Suddenly I knew it as sure as I know my own name—the man in black was a gangster! And he was going to steal Sam's father's motor home, kidnap us, and make our parents sell their houses to get us back.

"MONEY TIGHT? THAT'S OK!" the girls screamed.

The man turned towards me. Slowly, he pulled his hand out of the deep inner pocket of the coat. Something black waved in the air. It was about the size of a short ruler.

A scream gathered in my throat. I opened my mouth to let it out. It wrapped itself around my tonsils and stuck there. For a second I stared at him, frozen in place. Then something took over and sent me running. Darting between two Scotch pines, I clambered up over the fence and belly-flopped on the ground.

Help us God, I prayed, covering my head with both arms. *Bless this gangster and don't let him kidnap us. We've got a game on Saturday and it's almost Christmas.*

Footsteps followed me around the fence. *Please God, please God. Remember that electronic basketball game I wanted? Well, how about if we forget it?* Slowly, I brought my arms down and looked up—right into the blazing eyes of ...

Zack.

"Mick, what are you doing?" he demanded.

I got to my knees and looked around. The man in black was peering over the fence. He looked confused. I looked back at him, blinked, then looked again. Something I hadn't noticed before gleamed whitely above the inky blackness of his shirt. I gulped and covered my face with both hands.

My "gangster" was a pastor!

7

Wet behind the Ears

"I'm Pastor Willis from the big stone church up the street," the man said, looking down at me. "I'm sorry if I scared you. I have a nasty cold. I guess I sound gruff."

Behind him I could hear Trish and Brittany laughing. I struggled to my feet. My face felt redder than the lit end of a firecracker.

"A friend of yours sent me down here," he continued in his froggy voice. Now that I was standing up, he was acting like it was normal for Christmas tree sellers to jump over fences and dive to the ground. "Remember Tom Jackson? He lives at Meadowview," the man asked me. "Tom thought I could get some nice trees here for the church. We had terrible ones last year. I don't want to make a mistake like that again. I need six of your tallest spruce." He waved the black thing that had sent me running for cover. It was a checkbook.

My mind reeled. Six times $35 was—a lot. I tried to say something, but my voice still wouldn't work. Zack wrote up the sale, took the check, and tagged the trees for pick-up. I just stood there and stared.

"Thanks a lot," Pastor Willis croaked when he was done. He turned to me and smiled. "I'm really sorry about that scare, young man," he said.

"It's—it's OK," I managed to croak back.

When the pastor was safely back in his sleek black car, Zack looked at me and shook his head. "I don't know about you sometimes, Mick," he said.

I didn't know about me either.

"Don't pick on Mickey," Trish told Zack, tugging on her bright red baseball cap. "He just made us $210. If he hadn't been friends with Tom, it never would have happened."

"True," Zack agreed. He laughed. "Actually, it was kinda funny." He let out a scream, belly-flopped into a snowbank, and covered his head with his arms.

I laughed and belly-flopped down beside him. For a few seconds we rolled around, tossing snow at each other and shrieking. It may have been one of my dumber mistakes, but now that it was over, even I could see how funny it was.

"Hey! You offerin' credit now?" a voice by the market hollered.

Zack and I scrambled to our feet and turned

around. It was Dewey's mom, the lady who had said our trees cost too much that first day. She headed toward us, her puffy, gray coat flying out behind her like a cape.

"I just saw Pastor Willis here buyin' trees for the church," she said. "He's my pastor. If he's buyin', I figured maybe I ought to look again." Dewey's mom gazed at the Scotch pines I'd shown her earlier.

I dusted the snow off my jeans and walked over to meet her. All of a sudden I felt strong and in charge. "You can pick out a tree and we'll tag it for you, ma'am," I explained. "You can pay part today and the rest next week when you pick it up. If you water it right, I promise it won't get bald."

She pulled a long strand of flying hair away from her mouth. "That's good," she said. "I got Dewey to think about and all. OK, I'll take one of those $13 trees you showed me before. I get paid on Fridays, so I'll be back for it next Friday."

By the time our shift was over, we had down payments on four more $13 trees and two bigger ones. I couldn't wait to tell Tom. What I dreaded was telling him the part about Pastor Willis. I hoped he wouldn't think I was a big jerk.

"Want to go to Meadowview with me?" I asked Zack as we walked out onto Wooster Street.

Zack shook his head. "Can't. I'd like to, but I

haven't done my book report yet." He made a face. "Actually, I haven't even finished reading the book yet."

Zack was way ahead of me. I hadn't even *started* reading the book. "OK," I replied. "Tell Mom I'm visiting Tom and I'll be home in an hour."

At the nursing home I found Tom in his blue chair reading his Bible. His lips moved silently. When he sensed me standing in the doorway, he looked up and smiled. "So, you sell any trees?" he asked.

I broke into a grin and nodded. "Thanks to your great idea!" I told him, plopping down on the bed. "But first I have to tell you what happened with your pastor. You aren't going to believe this!"

By the time I finished the gangster story, Tom's gold tooth was flashing in the light. He pulled a bright white handkerchief from the pocket of his shirt and mopped his eyes. "The Good Book says there's a time to weep and a time to laugh," he chortled, "but I do believe this is a time for both! I haven't had such a good laugh since Miss Dulcie and Hairy Etta."

"Will you tell Pastor Willis that I'm not weird or anything?" I asked. I was glad he'd gotten such a kick out of it. I'd even acted out the part where I'd run for cover.

Tom nodded. "You can count on that," he promised. "There isn't anything weird about you, Mickey." He closed the Bible and shifted in his chair to see me better. "Now, tell me—how's the basketball coming?"

We'd been so busy with the tree problem I hadn't had time to sneak in any extra practice. And the big game against the Seville Pirates was only three days away. From what I heard, they had a not-so-secret weapon named Marcus Bennett. He could steamroll into a game and mow down guys the size of Sam Sherman.

"I don't know, Tom," I admitted. "Now that I'm a starter I'm really scared. Coach said if I do OK, he'll see about making it permanent. If I mess up, I could be out—just like Nick."

Tom's bushy, gray eyebrows squeezed together. "Why do you think you're not going to do good?" he demanded. "What's makin' you doubt yourself?"

That was easy. Yesterday in the locker room Sam Sherman had given me a look I'd only seen once before—the time we'd caught him taking the puppies from the church parking lot. It wasn't his usual put-down look. It was something a whole lot meaner. "Don't get too big for those little britches of yours, McGhee," he'd sneered. "You aren't one of us yet. And my money says you aren't going to be."

Tom sat still as stone in his blue chair while I talked. It was like I was the only person in the world he wanted to hear. When I was finished he didn't give me advice or tell me not to worry. He just said, "I do believe we need to pray on that," and closed his eyes. I closed mine too. He was quiet for so long I thought he'd fallen asleep.

"Dear Lord," Tom said suddenly.

I jumped at the sound of his voice.

"This boy here needs some belief in himself. He listened to the wrong person and now he's plumb forgot he can do all things in You. Help him please to walk in Your ways and delight in Your will. And then he won't have anything to worry about. Amen."

"Amen," I whispered. I opened my eyes. Tom's dark eyes were dancing like Meggie's when she's up to something.

"OK, we took care of the spiritual part," he said. "Now we have to take care of the practical. Open that closet over there and look on the floor to the right."

I got up off the bed and did what he said. On the floor I found a heavy cardboard box covered with an old, green plaid flannel shirt. "Move that shirt," Tom ordered.

Under the shirt a basketball sat in the middle of

a bunch of old books. The ball was so old its pebbled surface was worn smooth in spots. I picked it up and turned it around and around in my hands, holding it as carefully as if it were a cut-glass bowl on Grandma McGhee's Thanksgiving table. That ball had more games in it than I'd ever played in my life. Winning games. Losing games. Games that had made Tom's gold tooth flash. And games that hadn't.

"Let me see you dribble," he said.

I looked around, surprised. "Here?"

Tom nodded. "Go out there in the hall and let me see you move to the window."

It was a straight shot across the polished floor from the hall to the window of Tom's room. My dribbling skills weren't bad. Zack and I had practiced a lot, especially over the summer. I bounced the ball a few times and took off, beating it down hard. When I was done, I waited for his slow smile.

It didn't come. Tom shook his head. "Just what I was afraid of," he said. "You dribble that ball like you're trying to pound the air out of it. And you keep lookin' at it. Are you afraid it's goin' somewhere without you?"

I bounced the ball and caught it with both hands. I was confused. Nobody had ever said anything bad about my dribbling before. "I don't know what you mean," I said.

Tom used the arms of his chair to push himself to his feet. "Here, gimmee that ball," he said. "I'll show you."

I wasn't sure what the rules here at Meadowview were about old people playing basketball. But I handed over the ball and waited to see what would happen next. Tom walked out to the hall and bounced the ball. Then, faster than a ref calls "Foul!" he dribbled it across the floor. Never once did he look at it.

"You gotta dribble for a reason," he explained. He reached the window and turned around, still dribbling. "The dribble's not invented to show off your fancy tricks, it's to get you someplace. Too many young 'uns—and too many that should know better too—hog the ball so long the others on the team are just standin' around with nothin' to do. They get so bored they could knit themselves a sweater while they waitin'."

I laughed at that.

"Can you dribble with your left hand?" he asked.

I shook my head no. "Well, sort of," I corrected myself. "But I'm better with my right."

Tom shook his head. "You need to be better with both hands. And don't press down so hard. Spread your fingers, flex your wrist, and give it light pressure like this." Then he took off with the ball again. "And hold your head up so you can see where you're goin'," he added as he sailed through the door.

Outside in the hall a woman yelped. I ran to the doorway just in time to see a lady in a blue suit hurrying toward Tom. "Mr. Jackson! What on earth are you doing?" she cried.

I hoped Tom wouldn't get in trouble for helping me. "Afternoon, Miss Tracey," he greeted her. "I'm just showin' my young friend here a thing or two about basketball. I used to play a little back in the old days, you know." He winked at me like he and I were the only ones who knew he'd played pro.

Miss Tracey moved a clipboard from the crook of one arm to the other. "Well, I don't know if you're supposed to be exercising quite that much," she told him. Her bright pink mouth curved into a frown. "You be careful, OK?"

Tom nodded. "Don't you worry, Miss Tracey," he said softly. "I got what energy I got. And when it's gone, it's plumb gone and there's nothin' I can do about it. I reckon it's better to spend what's left doin' good than doin' nothin'."

Miss Tracey's cheeks turned pink. "Well, just be careful," she said, clicking down the hall in her high heels. I think she realized, like I did, that

Tom wasn't just talking about the energy he had today.

"Miss Tracey's the social worker," he explained when she'd turned the corner of the hall. "She's a good girl. Just wet behind the ears yet." He chuckled at that and touched a spot behind my right ear. "Just like you! Wet behind the ears."

He dribbled back into the room and sat down hard in his blue chair.

8

Walking the Plank

"Wow, did you see that Marcus Bennett?" LaMar asked in the locker room the day of the game against the Pirates. "He's HUGE, man. No way can that kid be our age. He makes that guy from the Blue Dolphins look like an elf."

Zack sighed. "I saw him. But he's our age all right. Coach knows his family. Man, he's gonna turn us into shredded wheat."

I was sitting next to Zack on the bench, changing my shoes and socks. Tom's prayer the day he'd taught me to dribble played like a tape in my head. "Hey, what kind of talk is that?" I asked, nudging Zack in the arm with my elbow. "We can win this thing; we've just gotta believe."

Sam Sherman jerked his head through the opening in his shirt and sneered. "The only thing I believe is that Coach is crazy to let a shrimp play against a guy as big as Bennett. You're gonna kill us out there, McGhee."

Zack jumped up, glaring. "Knock it off, Sam!" he growled. "Mickey's as good as any of us and you know it."

"Sure he is," LaMar agreed. "Knock it off, Sam. We're all nervous. Why don't we try to chill out, OK?"

A surge of doubt rose in my throat like acid. I knew I was a good player. But that Marcus guy was the biggest center we'd met yet. Tom's prayer flashed into my head again.

Usually, the time right before the game when both teams run around lobbing off balls is my favorite. Excitement crackles from the stands like electricity during a thunderstorm. With the air that full of possibility, anything can happen. But today I just wanted to get on with it. Every cell in my body felt primed and ready. I swallowed hard and followed the guys onto the court.

"And starting today for the Pinecrest Flying Eagles is Nummmmm-berrr 11, Mickey 'Spider' McGhee," the announcer yelled into the mike.

I scanned the crowd, found my family, and tossed them a grin. The sound of my name being read along with Sam's, Zack's, Luis', and LaMar's wiped out any lingering doubt. I'd waited too long for this chance to blow it now!

The game started fast and furious. Marcus Bennett led a stampede across the court and sank a two-pointer in 30 seconds flat. Sam Sherman muscled in for the turnover, but he was no match for the Pirates' center. Bennett whizzed in front of him and backed up to the basket, blocking hard. Sam zigzagged left and right, but Bennett's flailing arms held him back like a human dam. Sam aimed wildly and let go of the ball. It hit the backboard and bounced off.

Zack moved in and got the ball on the rebound. Bennett scooted around in front of him, forcing him to decide—shoot or pass. Zack passed to LaMar. LaMar whizzed the ball to me. I grabbed it and took off with Bennett so close on my heels I could hear him breathing.

I was cornered. I caught Sam Sherman's eye. His message was clear—"Pass, you turkey!" I tried. Suddenly something hard bashed me from the side. The next thing I knew I was staring up at the ceiling.

"Personal foul on number 23 of the Pirates, Marcus Bennett!" the announcer shouted.

Somewhere over my head a voice screeched, "I just bumped him! It's not *my* fault he's so little!"

Coach Duffy rushed out on the court and knelt down beside me. "You OK, Mickey?" he asked.

I was. At least I thought I was. I *had* to be! If I couldn't prove I could play with the big guys there was no room for me in basketball. Not now. Maybe not ever.

Little, frantic dots danced behind my closed

eyes. I blinked in the glare of the lights and struggled to sit up. The Pirates' coach was yelling and waving his arms at the ref. I forced myself to my feet and shook my head to clear out the fuzz. In the stands Mom looked ready to leap onto the floor. Dad gripped her arm, holding her down. I looked up and made my lips smile at her. She sat back down.

"Mickey? Can you play? You want to take some time out?" Coach asked.

"I'm fine," I answered. It was true. I was OK. My elbow burned, but it was just a red, angry scrape right on the surface. I blew on it to make the pain stop.

"HEY, HEY, TAKE IT AWAY! GET THAT BALL AND GO!" the cheerleaders shouted.

Like a cannonball I charged back into the game. By the end of the second quarter, I had scored six points and forced two turnovers. But the score stood at 14–26 in the Pirates' favor.

Slick with sweat, I jogged to the locker room and collapsed on a bench. Sam Sherman burst in behind me. He slammed his hand against a metal locker door. The sound made me jump a mile.

"This is crazy!" he cried. "I'm asking Coach to put Nick in and bench Shrimpo."

LaMar wiped his face on the towel draped around his neck. "Take it easy, Sam," he said.

"Mickey's doing fine. We can still win. It's a long way from over."

"No way!" Sam retorted. He was practically shouting now. "I'm talking to Coach! This has gone on long enough. Midgets don't play with giants."

"It's OK, Mick," Zack said quickly. He came over and sat down beside me. "Ignore him. He's acting like a jerk. Coach Duffy's the one who calls the shots."

That's exactly what I was afraid of. I'd played hard and done pretty well. But we were losing and I'd nearly been knocked out cold. If Sam pointed that out, Coach might just decide he was right. Tom's prayer shimmered in my head like sunlight on water. *He forgot he can do all things in You.*

The door opened and Coach Duffy barreled through. He was already barking orders. "OK, guys, same line-up for the second half! Watson, put some muscle into it this time. You too, Sherman. The big thing we have to do is ..."

"Lose the shrimp," Sam cut in.

Shock stood in the room like an extra person. Nobody talked that way to Coach Duffy. Ever.

Coach whipped around and looked at Sam. "What did you say?" he demanded.

"I said you need to bench Shrimpo," Sam repeated. The pink flush creeping up his neck told us he wasn't as sure of himself as he was acting.

Coach looked over at Nick. "Clemmons you're in. Sherman you're on the bench." The words stung like the snap of a wet towel.

"Whaaaat?" Sam squawked. "You can't do that! We'll lose! You need me!"

Coach Duffy shook his head. "The last thing we need in this game is somebody who can't be a team player. You're out."

I couldn't believe it! Not that Sam was benched. I was glad to see him cut down for once. He deserved it. What I couldn't believe was that I was almost sorry. If ever we needed Sam's size and strength, it was today!

Back out on the court, I turned it up a notch. So did everybody else. We scored some points and forced some turnovers, but we didn't have what it took to force a win. By the fourth quarter, the Pirates had us walking the plank. With less than a minute left on the clock, the handwriting was on the wall. I felt myself slowing down.

"Mick! Grab it!" Zack hissed from my left shoulder.

I looked where Zack was looking—just in time for Luis to shove the ball in my hands. My position was terrible. No way could I shoot from such a bad angle. I had to move in. In my head Tom's voice rapped out orders. *Eyes up. Look straight ahead. Light pressure. Move!*

Snaking in between two Pirates, I dribbled and aimed. Marcus Bennett lumbered over, arms waving. He jockied for position. I jockied back. Back and forth, back and forth, we sparred like a pair of boxers. And then I saw my chance. I aimed again and let it rip.

The ball arced in a perfect half-circle right over the top of Marcus Bennett's bobbing head.

"Beautiful!" the announcer cried as it dropped through the hole. "Too bad we can't see that in slow-mo! A perfect three-pointer by number 11 of the Flying Eagles, Spiiiiiiiiiiider McGhee!"

The buzzer shrilled. We lost 46–33.

9

A Call Is All

"Great shot, Mick!" LaMar said in the locker room. "That was awesome!"

I shrugged and muttered, "Thanks." It was a good shot. No question. But it might have been an accident. I wasn't sure. I hadn't been paying attention and all of a sudden I owned the ball. It probably didn't matter if it was luck or skill anyway. We'd still lost. And I'd been knocked flat in the first half.

In the lobby I found Mom and Dad. "Can you drop me at Tom's?" I asked. "I need to talk to him, OK?"

"Sure, honey," Mom replied, smoothing down the stick-up hair on top of my head. "You want us to wait for you?"

I shook my head no. "I'll walk home. This might take awhile."

I needed to talk to Tom so bad I thought we were never going to get to Meadowview. All the way in the car I could see myself pouring out the sad story of the game. But it wasn't pity I wanted.

It was an answer to the biggest question I had ever asked anybody in my whole life.

I found Tom sitting in his blue chair watching the Ohio State game on TV. I didn't say hi, or ask the score. I didn't even point out that OSU's center is my friend, Mike Sherman. The second I saw Tom, everything I felt bubbled to the surface and spilled out.

"We lost!" I cried, bursting into the room. "Why, Tom? Why did God let us lose? I believed just like you said, but we still lost. How could that be?"

Tom switched off the game. "Come sit down and tell me what happened," he said.

Only then did I realize how rude I'd been. I pointed to the TV. "Don't turn off the game because of me," I said, feeling my face get warm. "I can wait." I couldn't really, but I would just have to. It wasn't fair to break into Tom's fun, especially when Ohio State was winning.

Tom shook his head and turned in his chair to see me better. "There will be other games. Friends are always more important," he said firmly. "Now tell me what happened—real slow."

I told him how Marcus Bennett had knocked me down. And what Sam had said and how he'd gotten benched. And how I'd made that amazing shot over Bennett's head using my new dribbling skills. Never once did he try to hurry me up.

"I don't get it, Tom," I repeated when I was done. "How could God have let us lose?"

Tom reached over and placed a hand on my knee. "You think God let you down, is that it?" he asked. Before I could answer he said, "God didn't let you down. No, sir, He did not."

Tom leaned in closer. "You played a great game," he said. "Trouble is, you're makin' the same mistake lots of folks make. They think they're promised a win every time they pray. Now how are you ever going to learn anything if you get what you want every time you want it? It can't be done.

"The thing is, God's lookin' at the big picture and you're lookin' at the little one, Tom continued. "It doesn't matter whether you win this week or next week. What matters is you do your best and put your trust in Him. Then you don't have to worry about the little picture because you and God are partners in the big one. You understand what I'm sayin'?"

I was quiet for a few seconds, turning it all over in my brain. Finally I nodded. "I think so," I said slowly. "I think you're saying that God has a plan for me and I have to believe that He knows what's best. Right?"

Tom beamed. "You got it!" he said. "God uses

life to teach you. And sometimes what you need to learn is more important than what you want. You reckon you learned anything today?"

I thought about it. "Yeah, I think I did!" I cried, jumping up. It was like a light had flashed on in my brain.

"I really did!" I said. "I learned that I'm pretty tough. Even when I get knocked down I get right back up and go for it. Trouble is, I don't know whether or not Coach learned that." The light flickered and went out.

Tom chuckled. "I'm guessin' he did," he said. "But even if he didn't, you know it and God knows it. And that's all that matters in the big picture. Remember, it's the big picture that counts in the end. So you just keep your eye on that."

"I will," I promised. I wasn't sure whether or not I understood exactly what the big picture was. But it was a huge relief knowing that God and I were partners in it.

"Hey!" Tom said suddenly. He clapped his hands and grinned. "I almost forgot! We're havin' a Christmas party here tomorrow. You think you and Zack and Miss Dulcie might like to join us? And that nice dog of yours?"

"Sure," I said eagerly. "You want us to bring anything?"

Tom shook his head. "You just bring yourselves. That would be more than enough."

Zack agreed to come to the party. At first Dulcie was mad because Taco hadn't been invited, but she cheered up pretty quick. We found out why the next day when we went to pick her up. She came out on the porch wearing some kind of long dress under her jacket. A large, black garbage bag dangled from her hands.

"What's in the bag?" I asked as she climbed into the backseat with me and Zack.

"Angel wings," she answered.

"Angel wings?" I sputtered. "What do you need angel wings for? It's a party, not a play, for Pete's sake."

"I know that," Dulcie said like I was the one who was four years old. "But Christmas is baby Jesus' birthday. Just WHO do you think got invited to sing at the manger anyway, mister?"

"Uh—angels," I said. "But I don't think anybody said anything about singing."

Mom winked at me in the rearview mirror.

Dulcie sighed and clutched the garbage bag tighter. "You just don't get it, Mickey," she said.

She was right. I didn't. And if it involved her singing, I didn't WANT to get it!

Meadowview was buzzing with excitement. Carols poured out over the loudspeakers. A big table groaned under the weight of a zillion cookies. Plastic candles filled with liquid bubbled on the tree. And a happy crowd of old people and their families milled around, laughing and talking.

"Well, aren't you the sweetest little thing!" a lady with long gray hair gushed at Dulcie the second we walked through the door. She patted the gold garland wreath glittering in the fuzz on Dulcie's head. "Are you a little angel?" she asked.

"I'm one of the heavenly host," Dulcie said solemnly. She opened her garbage bag and wrestled the cardboard wings out. A shower of gold glitter rained all over the carpet.

I started to apologize for the mess, but Dulcie interrupted. "That's stardust," she said firmly. The lady laughed like it was the cutest thing since God made babies.

"Hey, there's Tom," Zack said, pointing to a chair next to the tree.

I hadn't seen him in the crowd. "Tom!" I called, heading over to him with Muggsy on a leash.

Tom's face lit up when he saw us. "Well look here," he cried. "Aren't I the lucky one! I've got so much company today! The Lord is good indeed!"

"Merry Christmas!" I said. "We brought ..." Before I could say "Muggsy," my dog jumped up on his lap and settled in.

"How about if I get us some cookies?" Zack asked, eyeing the snack table.

When Zack was gone, Tom grabbed my wrist and gave it a tug. "Lean down here a minute," he whispered. "I've got to ask you something."

I knelt down beside his chair and scanned the big room. People swirled around us in a blur of color and noise, but it was as if Tom and I were the only ones there.

Tom gripped my wrist tighter and pulled me in so my ear was right by his mouth. "I need your help," he said. "We've got a problem. We were supposed to have Santy Claus for the presents. And now we find that Santy Claus got the flu. We're going to have lots of unhappy people with no Santy at the Christmas party."

I looked around the big room. There were a few little kids dressed in their Sunday best, but most were my age or older. "Don't worry. That doesn't matter," I assured him. "Most kids won't care. And the little ones won't even know he was supposed to be here."

Tom laughed. "Oh, it's not the children I'm worried about." He looked around and put his finger to his lips. "It's the old folks! The old ladies sure do love their visit with Santy. We got the suit here. But what we don't have is a big man to fill it. You know anybody who might come down here and put that suit on?"

As a matter of fact I did. But I would rather sit on the bench than call *him*.

"Not really," I lied. I knew my face was redder than the stripes on a candy cane. I felt like a big fat rat. The perfect person was only one phone call away. All I had to do was dial—and I couldn't. Or wouldn't.

Tom looked at me and shook his head. "That's too bad," he said. "I was so hopin' you could help. Here comes Zack! Looks like we're gonna have a feast!"

Zack placed a plate heaped with cookies on the table next to Tom. My favorite sat on top like the crown on a queen. But not even peanut butter cookies with a whole Hershey's kiss stuck in the middle tempted me to dive in. Tom had helped us out with the tree sales. He'd taught me how to dribble right. He'd answered my questions about God. And now he wanted one little phone call and I was too selfish to make it.

"I just thought of somebody," I said suddenly.

Tom beamed as he looked up from his chair. "Somehow I knew you would!" he said. His eyes twinkled. He knew I'd been lying. He also knew who I was about to call.

10

Joy to the World!

My fingers shook as I pushed the buttons on the phone. I didn't know why I was so nervous. Wait! That's not true. I did know. But it was stupid. It wasn't like I was asking for anything for myself.

I explained how the Meadowview Santa had called at the last minute to say he had the flu. "So do you think maybe you could do it?" I finished. "I know it's kind of last minute. But it would mean a lot to everybody and …" My voice trailed off. He could probably tell my knees had turned to mashed potatoes.

"I think I might be able to," the voice on the other end of the phone said. "Oh, sure, why not? I'll be right down."

I hung up and ran back to Tom. "He said yes!" I reported. "He'll be right down."

Mrs. Wilkins, the activities lady, said she'd catch him at the side door before he came around front. He could put on the Santa suit and nobody would ever see him enter the building.

"Who are you talking about?" Dulcie asked, coming over to us. "Who is coming right down?"

"Santa Claus," Mrs. Wilkins answered.

Dulcie waved her arm in its floppy angel sleeve. "The angel of the Lord is more important than Santa Claus," she told us sternly.

Mrs. Wilkins smiled. "That's quite true," she replied. She winked at me and I grinned back.

"Come on, Dulcie," I said. "Let me help you with your wings." I wanted to get her away from the door, so she wouldn't see who was going to be wearing the Santa suit.

We found the wings leaning against the wall by the punch table. I helped her center them in the middle of her back. Zack held them in place while I tied the ribbons. When we were done Dulcie flapped her arms and spun in a circle. A lady in a wheelchair pushed hard against a white strap that was holding her in. She tried to say something, but no words came out.

Dulcie beamed a wide smile at her and hollered, "HI!"

The lady tried to speak again. This time a few sounds came out, but none of them made any sense. I gave her a shaky smile and looked around for Tom. I hoped I wasn't being rude. I just didn't know what to say or do.

Dulcie ran over and stood in front of the wheelchair. "I'm an angel," she said to the lady. "You like my costume, don't you?" She twirled in a circle so the woman could see the cardboard wings covered with gold glitter.

The woman nodded her head over and over. Tears misted her eyes, making them as shiny as tinsel. She reached out a hand and drew Dulcie closer. I watched in amazement as Dulcie gave her a quick hug and kept right on talking.

"Hey," Tom said behind me. "Looks like Miss Dulcie and Mrs. Baker are makin' friends."

I nodded. "It's like Dulcie's known her forever," I said. I didn't say anything about how dumb I'd felt just standing there smiling.

"Come over here and let's get some punch before Santy arrives," Tom said. I followed him to the punch table. He dipped a plastic ladle into the red liquid and carefully filled a cup for each of us.

"Thanks," I said, taking mine from his shaky hand. I was still watching Dulcie chattering away to the woman who couldn't talk.

Tom followed my gaze. "Mrs. Baker had a stroke a few months back," he explained. "Her brain knows what she wants to say, but her mouth doesn't get the message anymore. She's a great lady, Mrs. Baker. You know, she used to work in Washington, D.C. right on Capitol Hill with the president and all those important folks."

"Really?" My eyes widened as I watched her struggle to say something.

"That's so GOOD!" Dulcie squealed. "You said 'party'! Yes, this IS a party."

A loud crackle erupted over the loud speaker. "Welcome to Meadowview," Mrs. Wilkins' voice boomed. "We hope you're having a wonderful time this afternoon. We've just gotten word that we have a special visitor here today. A sleigh seems to have landed on our roof and ..."

"Santa Claus!" the little kids screeched, jumping up and down with excitement.

Mrs. Baker beamed from her wheelchair. I noticed that one of her arms didn't work any better than her voice did. She had to clap by hitting her right hand against the arm that lay in her lap. Dulcie leaned in and said something that made Mrs. Baker smile even wider. She put her working arm around Dulcie and drew her to her side. Dulcie rested her head on the old woman's shoulder.

Suddenly the front door burst open. A cold breeze whipped in behind a man in a red and white suit. "Ho! Ho! Ho!" he cried in a familiar voice. "Merrrrrrry Christmas!"

All eyes turned to watch as Santa Claus bounded into the party room. For a second he loomed in the doorway, studying the crowd of faces.

When he came to Mrs. Baker, he shouted "Ho! Ho! Ho!" and strode over to her. Mrs. Baker squealed and hugged Dulcie with her good arm. Two tears leaked out of her eyes and rolled down her face.

Santa reached into his pack and pulled out a present. "The first gift goes to Marybelle Baker," he read from the tag. "I heard she's been extra good this year." Gently, he placed a present wrapped in gold foil in the old woman's lap. It was tied with a big, red, floppy bow.

"Oh, that's so GOOD," Dulcie cried. She knelt down in front of Mrs. Baker. "I'll help you. We can do it together. I'll do the bow and you can tear the paper."

Santa Claus leaned over Dulcie's fuzzy head and planted a kiss right on Mrs. Baker's wet cheek! My eyes popped. I knew this Santa Claus. And he was not what I would call a kissing kind of guy. I looked at Tom, my eyes wide. He laughed. I knew he knew what I was thinking.

Santa stood up. "Tom Jackson?" he asked, striding over to where we were standing next to the punch bowl. For a second I wondered how he knew everybody's name. But then I remembered that Mrs. Wilkins had made name tags.

"That's me, Santy," Tom said with a grin. "I've been good as gold too." He nudged me with his elbow and laughed. "Well, at least as good as silver, I reckon."

Santa Claus chuckled and pulled out a box trailing curly green ribbons. He gave the box to Tom and handed me a package wrapped in blue. After we opened them I realized I hadn't brought a present for my new friend. "Tom, I didn't have time to get you anything yet," I apologized. "But I'll be back before Christmas and I'll bring it then."

Tom laid his hand on my arm and shook his head. "Haven't you already given me enough gifts?" he asked.

A woman sat down at the piano and began to play "Angels We Have Heard on High." Dulcie's ears pricked up like a cat's. She dropped her unopened gift in Mrs. Baker's lap and charged across the room like a torpedo.

Tom and I looked at each other and burst out laughing. We hunched up our shoulders and squeezed our eyes shut. We didn't have to wait long for what we knew was coming.

"GLOOOOO-OOOOOO-OOOOOO-OOO-OOOOOO-OOOOOOOOOOO REE-UH! IN EGGSHELL-SIS DAY-AY-O!"

We threw our arms around each other and laughed until we could have fallen on the floor.

"Ho! Ho! Ho!" roared Santa Claus. "What's this? Look what I've found! Way down deep in my pack! And just when I thought it was empty."

Tom and I broke apart and watched as Santa pulled a white envelope out of his burlap sack. He walked around the room, pretending to be looking for someone. "It says here Mickey McGhee," he boomed. "Where's Mickey McGhee?"

I knew he knew where I was, but I waved my hand and played along. Santa strolled over and handed me the envelope. I'd already had a present—a basketball novel from the series Zack and I both like a lot. Who could be giving me another gift?

"Is this from you?" I asked, turning to Tom.

Tom shook his head. "No, sir. I didn't have anything to do with it."

"Go on, open it," Santa ordered. He stood there watching as I carefully broke the seal and lifted the flap of the envelope. I read the front of the card, then opened it to the inside. There I read the special handwritten note. It said:

You're off to a great start, Mickey.
Let's keep it up. Merry Christmas!

I stared at the words. Did they mean ... *could* they mean what I thought they meant? I looked up and met Santa's eyes.

They were twinkling. "That's right," he said. "You're the new Pinecrest starter for the rest of the season! Ho! Ho! Ho! Merry Christmas!"

"Thhh-anks, Coach," I stammered. "I mean, thanks, Santa."

Beside me, Tom's wide smile turned his face into a road map of lines and creases. "What did I tell you?" he chortled. "The good Lord's got His eye on the big picture! He does indeed!"

"JOY TO THE WOOOOOOORLD!" Dulcie bellowed from across the room.

I couldn't have said it better myself.

Sixth Man Switch

TESS EILEEN KINDIG

One Extra-Large
Miracle to Go

Attention boys!
Basketball Teams Now Forming
Grades 4–6
Have Fun!
Make Friends!
Get Fit!

"Hey, look!" my best friend Zack Zeno shouted, pointing to the sign on the red brick wall of the city pool house. "Just what we've been waiting for!"

I shoved a weird black rock I'd found on the ground into the side pocket of my jeans and went over to check it out.

"Tryouts are Saturday morning," I read. "We're in, buddy!" I slapped him a high five and we pretended to do a jump shot.

Zack and I are total basketball freaks. Someday we're going to be high school hotshots. Then college all-stars. Then NBA pros. We've got it all planned. But until now we figured we'd have to wait until sixth grade to play on a real team.

"Hey!" somebody hollered from the parking lot next to the pool house.

It brought our feet down hard on the sidewalk. Every time I hear that voice I feel like I just got punched in the stomach. I could be at a real live Bull's game and the sound of that know-it-all tone would spoil the whole thing. Michael Jordan could sink a winning three-pointer and I'd be feeling sicker than the winner of a pie-eating contest.

"Hey, Sam!" I hollered back. I always pretend like Sam Sherman doesn't get to me. But it's getting harder and harder to do. Not only does he make my life miserable, but he also gets everything he wants. He even gets everything *I* want, which right now includes a dog and being tall enough to play center.

I know the last one will never happen, but I might actually get a dog someday. At least that's what my mom says. Trouble is, she's been saying it for two years already and "someday" is no closer than it ever was.

"You guys trying out for the team?" Sam asked. He came toward us, dribbling what looked like a brand new basketball. His huge black Lab, Zorro, pranced along beside him sporting a bright red collar.

"We might," Zack said.

"Yeah, we might," I agreed.

Sam dribbled the ball under his leg and lost control of it. It rolled off the sidewalk into the grass.

Zack and I grinned as he ran after it.

Sam picked up the ball and walked the rest of the way to the pool house. "You'd better get in some serious practice then," he warned. "Most of the guys who have a chance to make the team were at basketball camp this summer."

My heart sank. Well, not really. That's just a thing people say when they're upset. But if hearts *could* sink, mine would have ended up somewhere around my ankles. Sam was right. At the end of last year, a player from the local pro team came to our school and passed out flyers about the camp. Everyone who was serious about basketball signed up. Except for Zack and me. Basketball camp cost more than $100. Even without asking, we knew our parents couldn't afford it.

"We don't need basketball camp," I said now, heading toward my bike. "We're naturals."

"Naturals!" Sam scoffed. He laughed so hard he doubled up over the ball. "When's the last time you looked in the mirror, McGhee?" he asked me. "You're a little shrimp."

I picked up my bike from the ground where I'd crashed it and jumped on. Already I could feel my ears burning. It was like Sam Sherman held a remote control. All he had to do was press a button, and I turned as red as a sunburn. I'm the shortest boy in the fourth grade. Most of the *girls* are even taller than I am.

"Size doesn't matter," Zack said loyally, jumping on his bike too. "Mickey's got speed."

I didn't say anything. Sam was showing off his crossover dribble. It was so fast and clean, you could set it to music. He'd sure learned a lot at that basketball camp.

Zorro barked and ran in little circles as the ball bounced across the concrete. Usually I like to watch Zorro, but not today. I rode off toward home with Zack behind me. We didn't talk until we crossed the street and were safely in our own neighborhood. Then he rode up alongside me.

"Don't let him get to you," he said. "We're in. We're in!"

"I know," I agreed. But I wasn't so sure anymore.

At my house, I turned onto the bumpy gravel driveway and Zack followed. Our old ten-speeds rattled like two jars of marbles. We squeezed our handbrakes and came to a stop, sending the gravel flying.

"Want to do a little one-on-one before supper?" Zack asked.

"OK." I dropped my bike and got my basketball from the garage. I'd told my mom I'd clean my room after school, but maybe if I didn't go into the house, she'd forget for awhile.

I bounced the ball a few times on the pad by the side door of the house. The thud, thud, thud sound it made slapping against the fresh concrete made my muscles unclench. My dad and I had just poured that pad two weeks ago. We built the frame and everything. When the cement was ready, Dad mounted a metal pole in the ground to hold the basket. Later Zack and I painted it black. Nobody could even tell it used to be a city lightpole we got for free.

I tossed the ball to Zack and he pivoted wildly in all directions, trying to freak me out.

"Dee-fense! Dee-fense!" I shouted, trying to block with my arms.

Zack laughed and shot over my head. The ball hit the rim and bounced off. We both scrambled for it.

"Hi, Mickey!"

I froze, both hands on the ball. There's only one other voice besides Sam Sherman's that can stop me cold, and this was it. I let go of the ball and straightened up.

"Hi, Trish," I said.

Trish Riley lives down the street and sits in front of me in Mrs. Clay's class. It's totally embarrassing to admit this, but she has a monster crush on me. I hate it. Neither Zack nor I want to get involved with girls. At least not until we're 27. Maybe even 30!

She pulled the brim of the baseball cap she always wears down over her forehead and smiled. "You're really good, Mickey. I bet you make the team."

Zack pretended like he was practicing his speed dribble. But I could see his shoulders shaking up and down from laughing. Good? What did Trish Riley know about good? I'd just let Zack complete a throw that should have gone in easy.

"Thanks." I turned back to Zack, but Trish made no move to leave.

"I guess you heard about Sam Sherman," she said.

"What about him?" I could feel my muscles tensing up again.

Now that she had my attention, Trish walked up the driveway. "Last Saturday he landed a pair of baskets in front of 2000 people at an exhibition game."

"Huh?" Suddenly I was all ears.

She nodded. "It's true. He went up to State to see his brother play. His brother's a big star at the university, you know."

Zack stopped dribbling and came over. "Sam Sherman didn't play at any State game," he said. "No way. No way!" But you could tell he wasn't sure.

Now that she had Zack's attention too, Trish continued her story. "Yes, he did," she said, yanking on her baseball cap again. That's something she does whenever she talks to me. "At halftime they toss T-shirts into the crowd. If you catch one, you get to go down on the floor and shoot. Sam grabbed one, raced down there and shot two baskets right in a row. No misses."

Zack and I exchanged glances. I knew he was thinking the same thing I was. *How thrilling it would be to hear the crowd roaring its approval, especially for a fourth grader.*

"Oh yeah? So what?" I said, reaching down for the ball Zack had left on the ground.

Trish saw she was losing us. "He won a real prize too," she

added. "Got a whole wad of coupons for free food. Burgers, shakes, fries, all kind of free stuff."

We let that sink in. Rarely did we get to eat fast food. I couldn't even remember when I'd last wrapped my mouth around a bacon cheeseburger. But that wasn't the important part. The big thing was Sam Sherman out on the court shooting baskets at a college game.

Zack and I looked at each other again. We didn't even have to say it.

We were dead.

Behind me a window squeaked open on the side of the house. "Mickey McGhee! You get in here and clean your room this minute!" my mom shouted.

Red crawled up my neck and stained my face like cherry Kool-Aid. "I gotta go," I mumbled.

I picked up my bike, tossed the basketball in the dented wire basket and wheeled the bike up the driveway to the garage. "See ya, Zack!" I called. I didn't say good-bye to Trish. It's not that I was trying to be rude or anything. I just didn't want her getting any more ideas than she already had.

Our garage is only big enough for one car. So I always have to make sure to get my bike tight against the wall so my dad doesn't drive his pickup into it. I did that, then walked back toward the house.

In my head I could hear the college band playing "Hang On Sloopy" during halftime. I could smell the nachos and taste the icy blast of freshly poured pop. But mostly, I could feel the excitement crackling like wrapping paper around an Easter basket, as Sam Sherman strutted his stuff on the wide, polished floor.

It made me groan right out loud. We were only kidding ourselves. For Zack Zeno and Mickey McGhee to land a spot on the basketball team it was going to take a miracle!

On the scale of, say, the loaves and the fishes. Or the wedding feast of Cana.

In other words, a real doozy!

Only Jesus could pull off something that big!

Sixth Man Switch

"It made me groan right out loud. We were kidding ourselves. It was going to take a miracle for Zack Zeno and Mickey McGhee to land a spot on the basketball team."

Fourth-grader Mickey McGhee and his best friend, Zack Zeno, eat, sleep, and breathe basketball. When the city announces a basketball league for their age group, they are thrilled.

But Sam Sherman and his friends plan to try out as well; no doubt they will be using height and fast new moves to score important spots on the team. What chances do these two friends have against taller fellow athletes who trained at a pro basketball camp? A lot!

Spider McGhee and the Hoopla

"I'm looking for the little guard," said Dave Dawson from the Gazette. "Number 11. There he is! Hey kid, where'd you learn to play b-ball like that?"

When fourth-grader Mickey McGhee becomes the surprising basketball dynamo in the city league, everybody notices, including the media. Because of his speed and dexterity, he earns the nickname "Spider" and a following of fans.

But Mickey forgets something in all the media excitement and hype that nearly ruins it all. He learns the importance of friendship, forgiveness and unconditional love—especially God's love.

Zip Zero Zilch

"I knew Mom was right about God and love and all that. But right now I felt too crummy to listen. When was I going to get to be the neighbor everybody was supposed to love?"

Sam Sherman's game is hotter than ever! He just can't seem to miss! Since Mickey's plays aren't getting any attention at all, he decides to make some game adjustments. And he gets plenty of attention—just the wrong kind!

Through it all, Mickey learns that responsibility to God, his friends, family, and himself is more important than scoring points or winning games. Read along as Mickey puts his faith into action.

Muggsy Makes an Assist

"I laughed so hard I dropped Muggsy's leash and fell against the wall, holding my sides. Then I saw my dog fly around the corner so fast it looked like all four paws were off the ground. 'Muggggseeee!' I called, dashing down the hall."

If Mickey could eat, sleep, and drink basketball, he would. There is nothing he would rather do than play one game and think about the next one.

But as Mickey focuses more and more on his basketball game, he has less time to concentrate on other things—even his new dog Muggsy is left out in the cold. But Mickey discovers a need to balance his priorities and concentrate on the important stuff. Read on to discover what